MORE GREAT GRAPHIC NOVELS FROM

PAPERCUTZ™

THE SMURFS #21

FUZZY BASEBALL #1

FUZZY BASEBALL #2

THE SISTERS #1

TROLLS #1

GERONIMO STILTON #17

THEA STILTON #6

SEA CREATURES #1

DINOSAUR EXPLORERS #1

SCARLETT

ANNE OF GREEN BAGELS #1

DRACULA MARRIES FRANKENSTEIN!

THE RED SHOES

THE LITTLE MERMAID

BARBIE #1

HOTEL TRANSYLVANIA #1

THE LOUD HOUSE #1

MANOSAURS #1

THE ONLY LIVING BOY #5

GUMBY

SEE MORE AT PAPERCUTZ.COM

Fuzzy Baseball

John Steven Gurney

PAPERCUTZ

Fuzzy Baseball 2

NINJA BASEBALL BLAST

John Steven Gurney

PAPERCUTZ
New York

Fuzzy Baseball #2
"Ninja Baseball Blast"
Created by JOHN STEVEN GURNEY
MANOSAUR MARTIN—Production
KARR ANTUNES—Editorial Intern
JEFF WHITMAN—Managing Editor
JIM SALICRUP
Editor-in-Chief

Hardcover ISBN: 978-1-5458-0008-9

Paperback ISBN: 978-1-5458-0366-0

Printed in India
May 2019
Papercutz books may be purchased for business or promotional use.
For information on bulk purchases please contact
Macmillan Corporate and Premium Sales Department at
(800) 221-795 x5442.

Distributed by Macmillan
First printing

FERNWOOD VALLEY FUZZIES

BO "THE GRIZ" GRIZZLY

34
FIRST BASE

FERNWOOD VALLEY FUZZIES

HAMMY SOSA

21
CATCHER

FERNWOOD VALLEY FUZZIES

JACKIE RABBITSON

42
CENTERFIELD

FERNWOOD VALLEY FUZZIES

SANDY KOFOX

32
PITCHER

FERNWOOD VALLEY FUZZIES

BLOSSOM HONEY-POSSUM

1 / 8
OUTFIELD

FERNWOOD VALLEY FUZZIES

KIT OCELOT

45
PITCHER

FERNWOOD VALLEY FUZZIES

LARRY BOA

10
THIRD BASE

FERNWOOD VALLEY FUZZIES

PERCIVALE PENGUINO

7
OUTFIELD

FERNWOOD VALLEY FUZZIES

PEPE PERRITO

13
SECOND BASE

FERNWOOD VALLEY FUZZIES

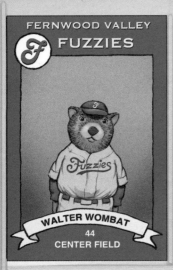

WALTER WOMBAT
44
CENTER FIELD

SASHIMI CITY

14
RIGHT FIELD

ANDRES GALAGO

NINJAS

FERNWOOD VALLEY FUZZIES

KAZUKI KOALA
19
RIGHT FIELD

SASHIMI CITY

AYANO ANOLE

INFIELD

43

NINJAS

FERNWOOD VALLEY FUZZIES

PONY PEREZ
24
SHORTSTOP

SASHIMI CITY

55

NICO MANEKI

PITCHER

NINJAS

FERNWOOD VALLEY FUZZIES

PAM THE LAMB
8
LEFT FIELD

SASHIMI CITY

9

CENTER FIELD

ICHIRO IGGLE

NINJAS

FERNWOOD VALLEY FUZZIES

RED KOWASAKI
29
PITCHER

SASHIMI CITY

PUG RODRIGUEZ

CATCHER

11

NINJAS

SASHIMI CITY

MELVIN OTTER

SECOND BASE

5

NINJAS

SASHIMI CITY

62

SHORTSTOP

YUKI SKIRL

NINJAS

SASHIMI CITY

IGNACIO IGUANA

LEFT FIELD

8

NINJAS

SASHIMI CITY

TOMIKO TAMARIN

PITCHER

15

NINJAS

SASHIMI CITY

4   MUTSUMI MUTT

OUTFIELD

NINJAS

SASHIMI CITY

HIDEKI HEDGEHOG

THIRD BASE

27

NINJAS

SASHIMI CITY

32   HIROSHI HOP

FIRST BASE

NINJAS

SASHIMI CITY

7   SATOSHI SQUID

THIRD BASE

NINJAS

EIGHT HOURS LATER, THE FUZZIES ARRIVE IN SASHIMI CITY...

19

23

25

THERE ARE MANY DIFFERENT TYPES OF PITCHES IN MANGA BASEBALL.

THE CRISS-CROSS TURTLE

THE BOWLING DONKEY

THE SPRINGY SALAMANDER

THE HIGH STEP TOUCAN

THE SLEEPY MOUSE

THERE ARE MANY FUN WAYS TO HOLD THE BAT IN MANGA BASEBALL.

CHOP-CHOP SWING

JAZZY SWING

BUTTS UP SWING

HAPPY SWING

IT'S TOO HIGH
FOR TOMIKO....

BUT NOT TOO HIGH FOR YUKI!
THAT'S OUT NUMBER ONE.

THE NEXT BATTER WAS
PERCIVALE PENGUINO...

WHERE DID THAT CRAZY
ITALIAN PENGUIN GO?

KAZUKI SLICES THE BALL DOWN THE RIGHT FIELD LINE...

THE GRIZ SCORES FROM SECOND!

AND HAMMY SCORES FROM FIRST! THE FUZZIES TAKE THE LEAD!

SAFE!

SAFE!

AZUKI IS SAFE AT THIRD. NEXT UP: LARRY BOA...

DO YOU THINK IT'S TIME?

I THINK IT'S TIME!

THE MEETING CONTINUES IN THE NINJA DUGOUT...

THE CROWD STARTS TO CHANT...

MASTER KOMODO PRESENTS THE MORFO BALL TO TOMIKO...

41

IN MANGA-BASEBALL YOUR MORFO-POWER BLAST **POWER LEVEL** IS BASED ON YOUR **PASSION FOR BASEBALL!**

LARRY AND THE NEXT BATTER STRIKE OUT TO END THE TOP OF THE SECOND INNING...

THE NINJAS ARE UP.... *HIDEKI HEDGEHOG* STEPS UP TO THE PLATE....

MORFO POWER BLAST!

THAT JUST DOESN'T SEEM FAIR.

POWER LEVEL 4

HIDEKI HITS A HOME RUN!

THAT'S MANGA BASEBALL.

CRACK.

AYANO ANOLE HITS A HOME RUN....

I WISH WE COULD USE THAT MORFO BALL.

CRACK

POWER LEVEL 7

KIT CALLS FROM THE PITCHER'S MOUND...

HEY, HAMMY, TOSS IT BACK TO ME!

MORFO POWER BLAST!

POWER LEVEL 6

WHEN THEY GET THIS BIG, I CAN'T EVEN SEE!

THE END

INSTANT REPLAY

A MEMO FROM THE COMMISIONER

Baseball was introduced to Japan from America around 1870. In "Ninja Baseball Blast" I wanted to celebrate many of the fun things that our culture has imported from Japan. The Fuzzies meet ninjas, try sushi, learn from a manga style textbook, and even encounter a giant kaiju (Godzila is an example of a famous kaiju).

I also wanted to have some fun with the idea of transformation. In Japanese influenced shows, cars transform into giant robots, rangers morph into mighty warriors, and little pocket monsters evolve into larger pocket monsters. In English literature, Alice goes through many transformations in Wonderland, and Dr. Jekyll transforms into Mr. Hyde. In American movies, people transform into werewolves and superheroes all the time. Even Bugs Bunny transforms (when he meets Dr. Jekyll).

As a child, my drawing style was influenced by cartoons created by Walt Disney and Warner Bros. Today, the drawing style of American school children is often influenced by Japanese comics which were created by Japanese artists who grew up watching those same American cartoons (among so many other influences as well). It's amazing the way a culture can absorb an influence from across the globe and transform it into something unique.

I hope you enjoyed reading about the Fuzzies' wacky, and transformative, encounter with another culture.

John Steven Gurney

WATCH OUT FOR PAPERCUTZ™

Even though FUZZY BASEBALL #1 was clearly a homerun, we're just now making it to second! The second FUZZY BASEBALL graphic novel, that is. Welcome to the second, screwball FUZZY BASEBALL graphic novel, by John Steven Gurney (learn more about the talented Mr. Gurney at johnstevengurney.com), from Papercutz, those FUZZY BASEBALL season ticket holders dedicated to publishing great graphic novels for all ages. I'm Jim Salicrup, Editor-in-Chief and Technical Error collector.

In "Ninja Baseball Blast," we see the Fernwood Valley Fuzzies battle the Sashimi City Ninjas, and as exciting as that classic encounter turned out, now I'm wondering what games against other Papercutz superstars would be like. For example, the Fuzzies would have a great advantage playing against THE SMURFS. After all, the Smurfs are only three apples, or baseballs, tall. Probably the only Smurf able to lift a regulation-size bat would be Hefty Smurf. Unless Papa Smurf came up with some kind of magical spell, I'm betting the Fuzzies would clobber the Smurfs.

On the other baseball-gloved hand, Lincoln Loud and his ten sisters, Lori, Leni, Luna, Luan, Lynn, Lucy, Lola, Lana, Lisa, and Lily, the stars of the hit Nickelodeon TV series THE LOUD HOUSE and of their own Papercutz graphic novel series, stand a much better chance against the Fuzzies. The Fuzzies would probably still easily win, they are a real baseball team, after all, but I wouldn't underestimate Lynn Loud's sports skills and ability to whip her team into shape—she has more than enough siblings to put together an all-Loud line-up, although Lily may be a little too young to play.

A much tougher team might be made up from the stars of THE ONLY LIVING GIRL (The exciting follow-up graphic novel series to THE ONLY LIVING BOY). With just two human players, Zee and Erik, and a bunch of mutants and monsters, this team will pack a wallop, if not a lot of finesse. If Erik can swing a bat as well as he does his wooden sword or if Morgan Dwar focused her considerable combat skills, they could possibly pull off a surprise upset.

Another power-hitting dream team could be composed of the combined casts from MANOSAURS and DINOSAUR EXPLORERS. Just imagine a team with humans, dinosaurs, and human/dinosaur hybrids! While some of the dinosaurs may not grasp the concept of baseball, how could you not want a real-life raptor on your team? How DINOSAUR EXPLORERS' Rain, Emily, Sean, and Stone would get along with MANOSAURS' Tri, Rex, Ptor, and Pterry is another story. (Check out the preview of DINOSAUR EXPLORERS #1 on the following pages, if you haven't picked up their great graphic novels yet!)

But the team I'm probably most excited about is the gang from THE HOTEL TRANSYLVANIA (the stars of the hit movies, animated TV series, and Papercutz graphic novels)! This would definitely be loads of fun to watch. Not necessarily to witness a well-played game, but just to see how wild and wacky things would get. THE HOTEL TRANSYLVANIA would even have three players (Mavis, Drac, and Vlad) that can literally turn into bats. Not baseball bats, but bats! And who could possibly steal bases better than the Invisible Man?

Who knows what really awaits the Fernwood Fuzzies next? Who could've guessed they'd play against ninjas? Probably John Steven Gurney knows, but he's not telling. We'll just have to wait for the next FUZZY BASEBALL graphic novel to find out.

Thanks,

JIM

STAY IN TOUCH!

EMAIL:	salicrup@papercutz.com
WEB:	papercutz.com
TWITTER:	@papercutzgn
INSTAGRAM:	@papercutzgn
FACEBOOK:	PAPERCUTZGRAPHICNOVELS
REGULAR MAIL:	Papercutz, 160 Broadway, Suite 700, East Wing, New York, NY 10038

Here's a special preview of DINOSAUR EXPLORERS #1 "Prehistoric Pioneers"...

YES! WE HAVE BEEN SENT 570 MILLION YEARS INTO THE PAST!

INTO THE CAMBRIAN PERIOD!

GASP

NGYAH!

YOU MEAN WE ALL CAME FROM THAT -- THAT FIVE-EYED THING?!

IT'S CALLED AN "OPABINIA," BY THE WAY. AND WELL, EVOLUTION IS A FUNNY THING. MIND YOU, THERE ARE A LOT OF OTHER CANDIDATES FOR YOUR GREATEST GRANDFATHER AS WELL; MANY ARE SINGLE-CELLED ORGANISMS, WHILE A LOT OF OTHERS LACK BACKBONES.

ANIMALS WITH SKELETONS AND BACKBONES ARE CALLED VERTEBRATES.

ANYTHING WITHOUT A BACKBONE IS AN INVERTEBRATE-- AND NO, SHELLS DON'T COUNT.

I READ THAT SINCE MANY TRILOBITE FOSSILS COME FROM THE CAMBRIAN, THIS PERIOD IS ALSO KNOWN AS--

The Trilobite Era!

OOOH! DOES THAT MAKE US THE FIRST HUMANS IN THE CAMBRIAN PERIOD?

Aha!

Don't miss DINOSAUR EXPLORERS #1, available now at booksellers everywhere.